THE TELL-TALE HEART

Adapted by

Joeming Dunn

Illustrated by

Rod Espinosa

Based upon the works of

Edgar Allan Poe

magic
Wagon

visit us at
www.abdopublishing.com

Published by Magic Wagon, a division of the ABDO Publishing Group, 8000 West 78th Street, Edina, Minnesota 55439.

Printed in the United States

Manufactured with paper containing at least 10% post-consumer waste

Adapted by Joeming Dunn
Illustrated by Rod Espinosa
Colored and lettered by Rod Espinosa
Edited by Stephanie Hedlund and Rochelle Baltzer
Interior layout and design by Antarctic Press
Cover art by Rod Espinosa
Cover design by Neil Klinepier

Library of Congress Cataloging-in-Publication Data

Dunn, Joeming W.
The tell-tale heart / adapted by Joeming Dunn ; illustrated by Rod Espinosa ; based upon the works of Edgar Allan Poe.
p. cm. -- (Graphic planet. Graphic horror)
Summary: A graphic novel based on the Edgar Allan Poe classic, in which the murder of an old man is revealed by the continuing beating of his heart.
ISBN 978-1-60270-681-1 (alk. paper)
1. Graphic novels. [1. Graphic novels. 2. Murder--Fiction. 3. Guilt--Fiction. 4. Crime--Fiction. 5. Poe, Edgar Allan, 1809-1849. Tell-tale heart--Adaptations. 6. Horror stories.] I. Espinosa, Rod, ill. II. Poe, Edgar Allan, 1809-1849. Tell-tale heart. III. Title.
PZ7.7.D86Tel 2010
741.5'973--dc22

2009008589

TABLE OF CONTENTS

The Tell–Tale Heart.................. 4

About the Author.................31

Additional Works..................31

Glossary.............................. 32

Web Sites............................. 32

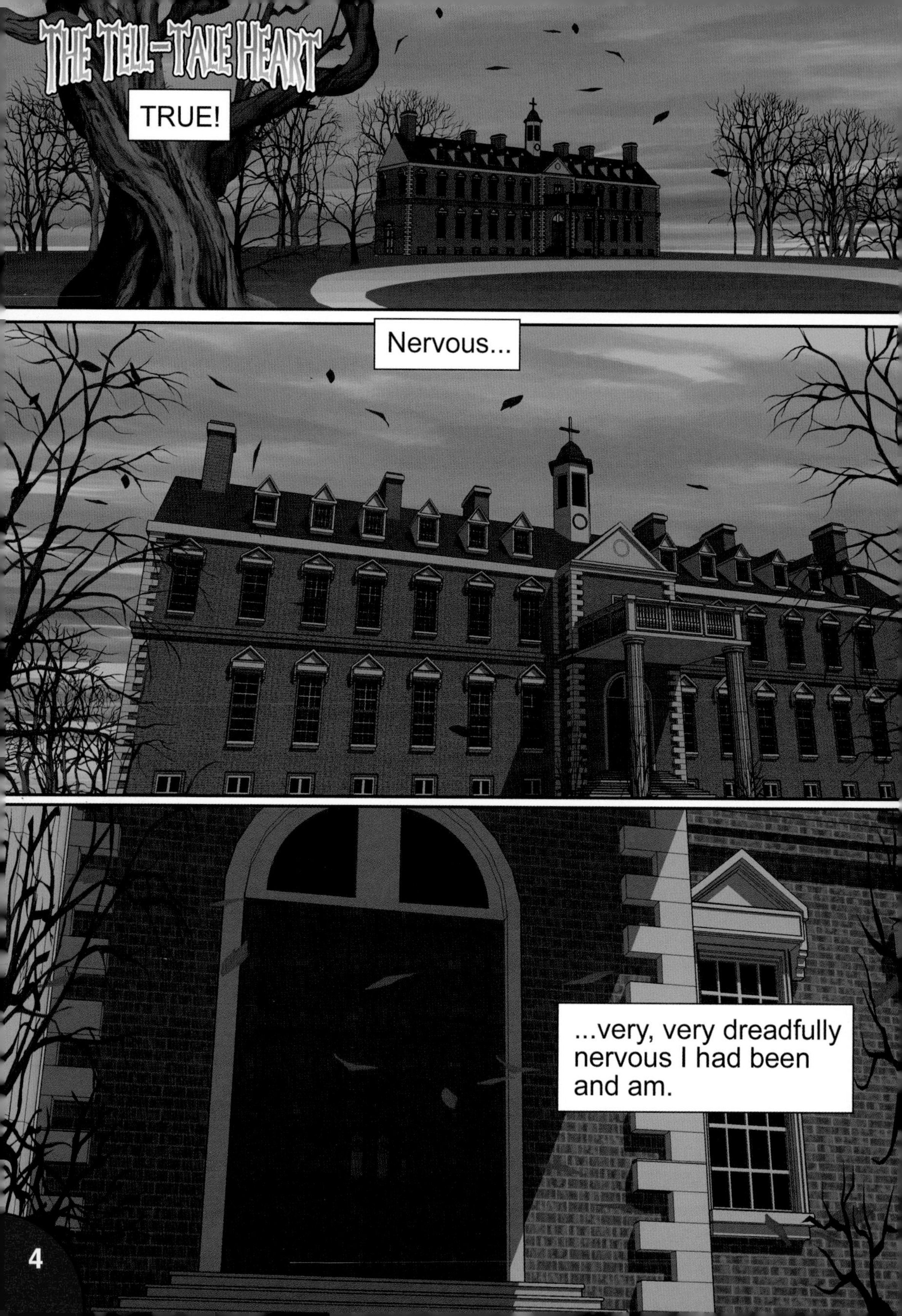
THE TELL-TALE HEART
TRUE!
Nervous...
...very, very dreadfully nervous I had been and am.

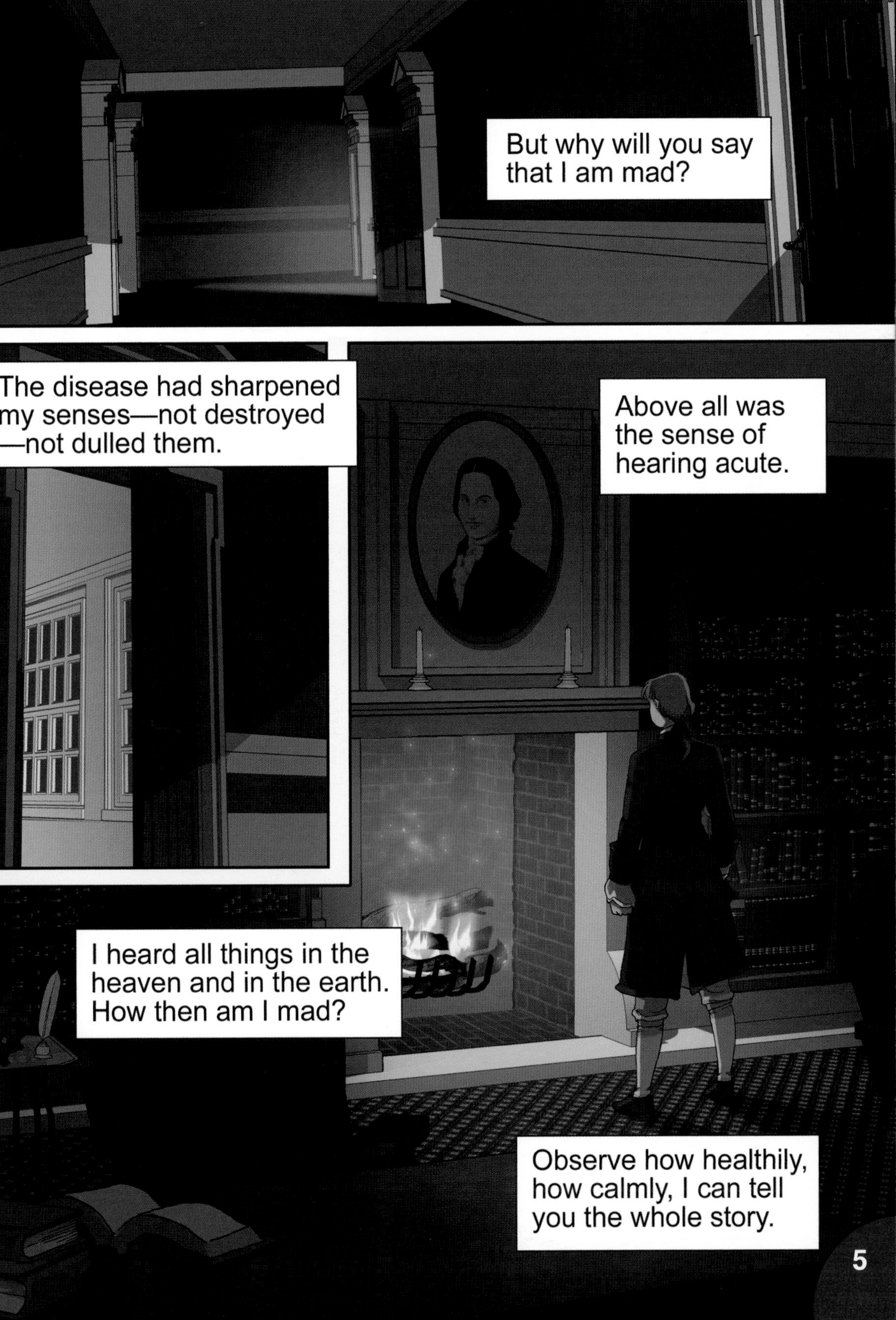
But why will you say that I am mad?
The disease had sharpened my senses—not destroyed—not dulled them.
Above all was the sense of hearing acute.
I heard all things in the heaven and in the earth. How then am I mad?
Observe how healthily, how calmly, I can tell you the whole story.

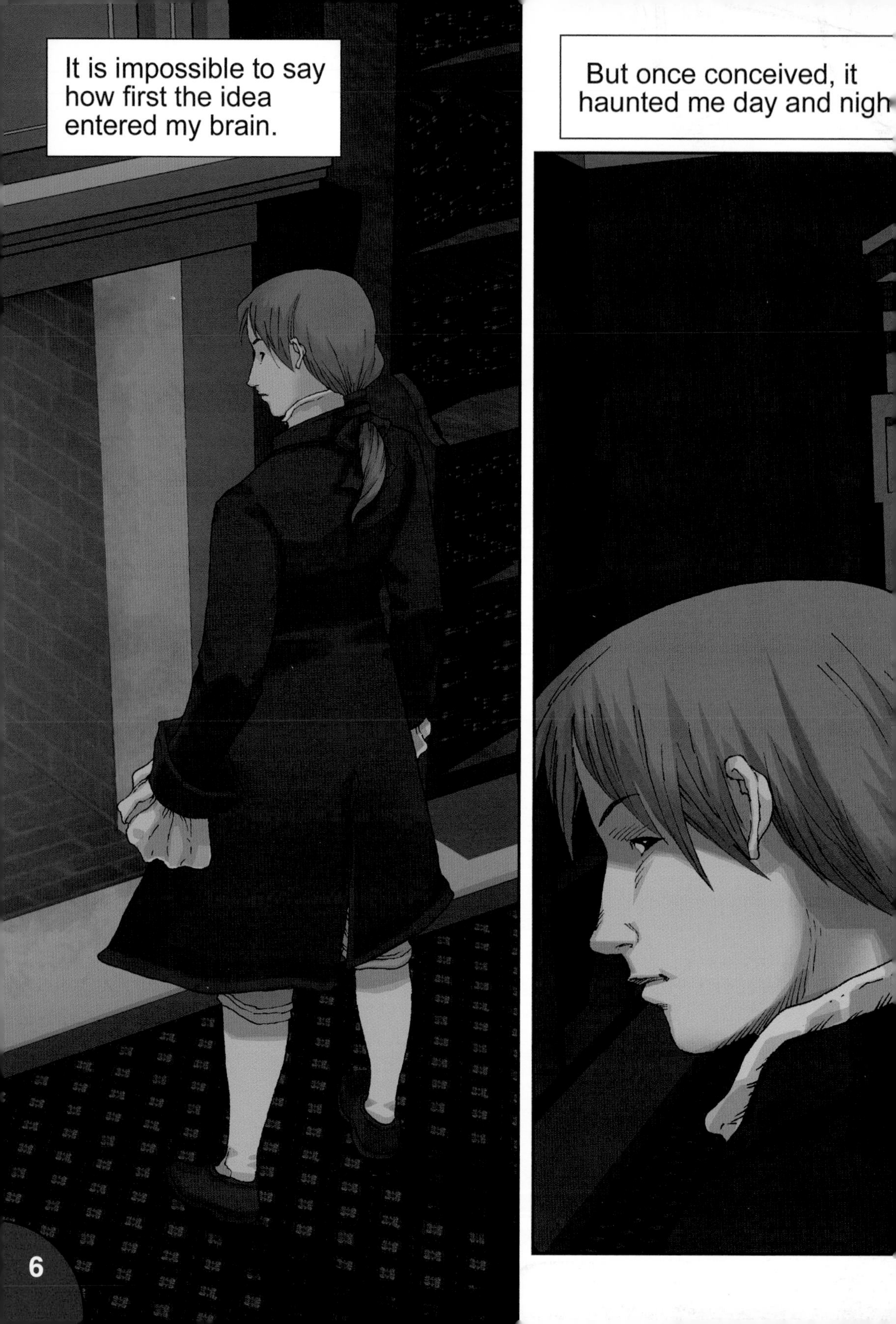
It is impossible to say how first the idea entered my brain.
But once conceived, it haunted me day and nigh

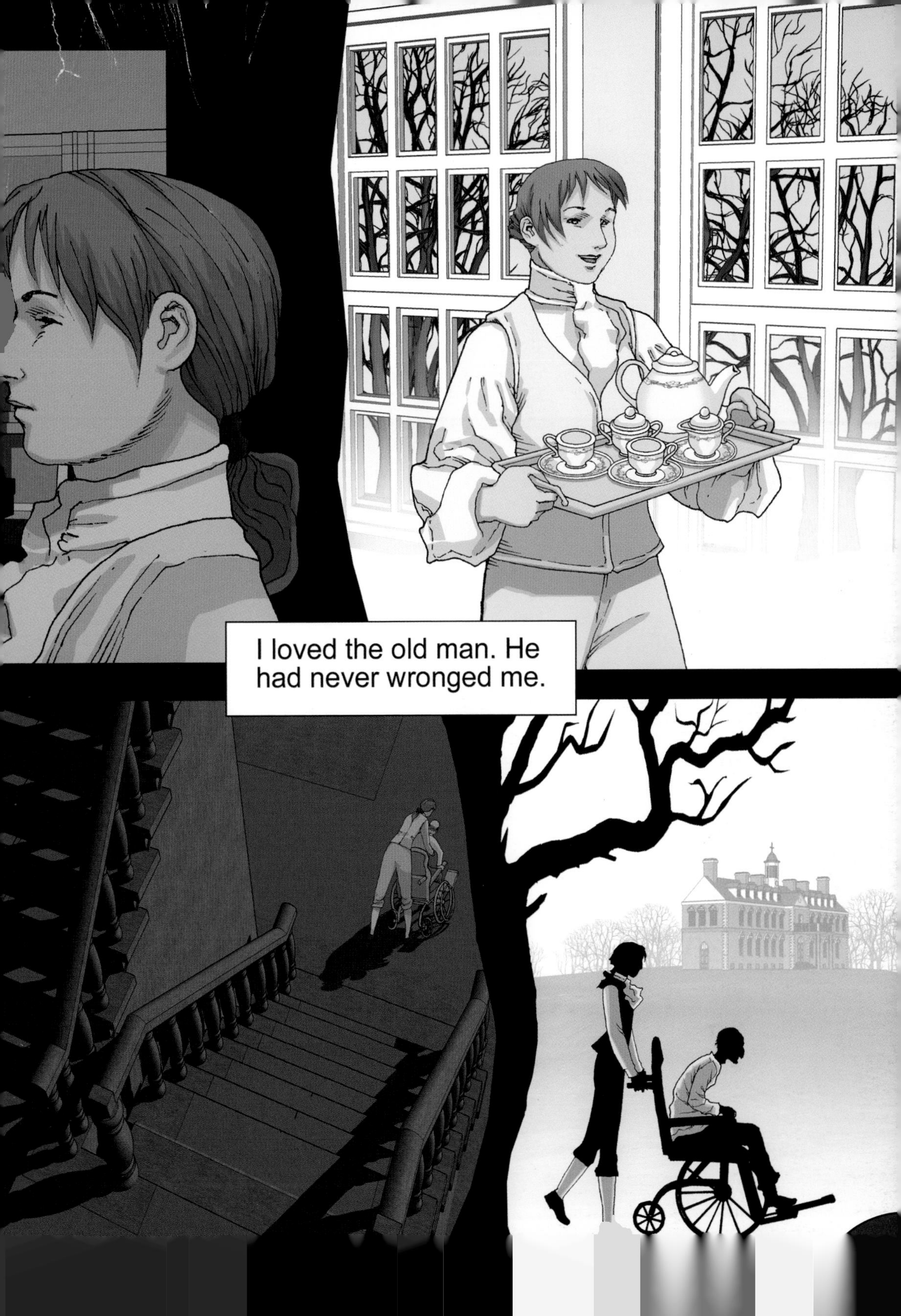
I loved the old man. He had never wronged me.

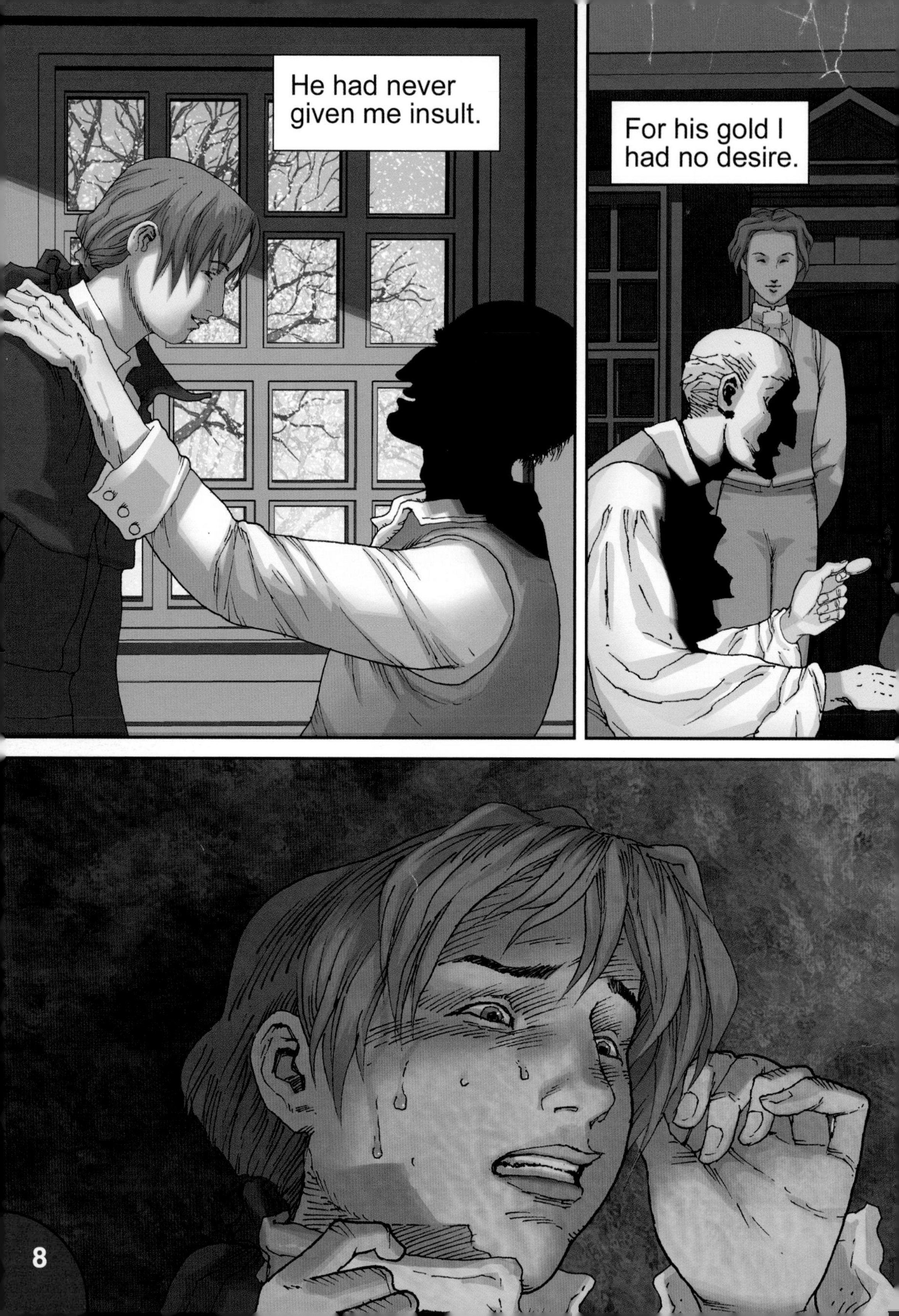
He had never given me insult.
For his gold I had no desire.

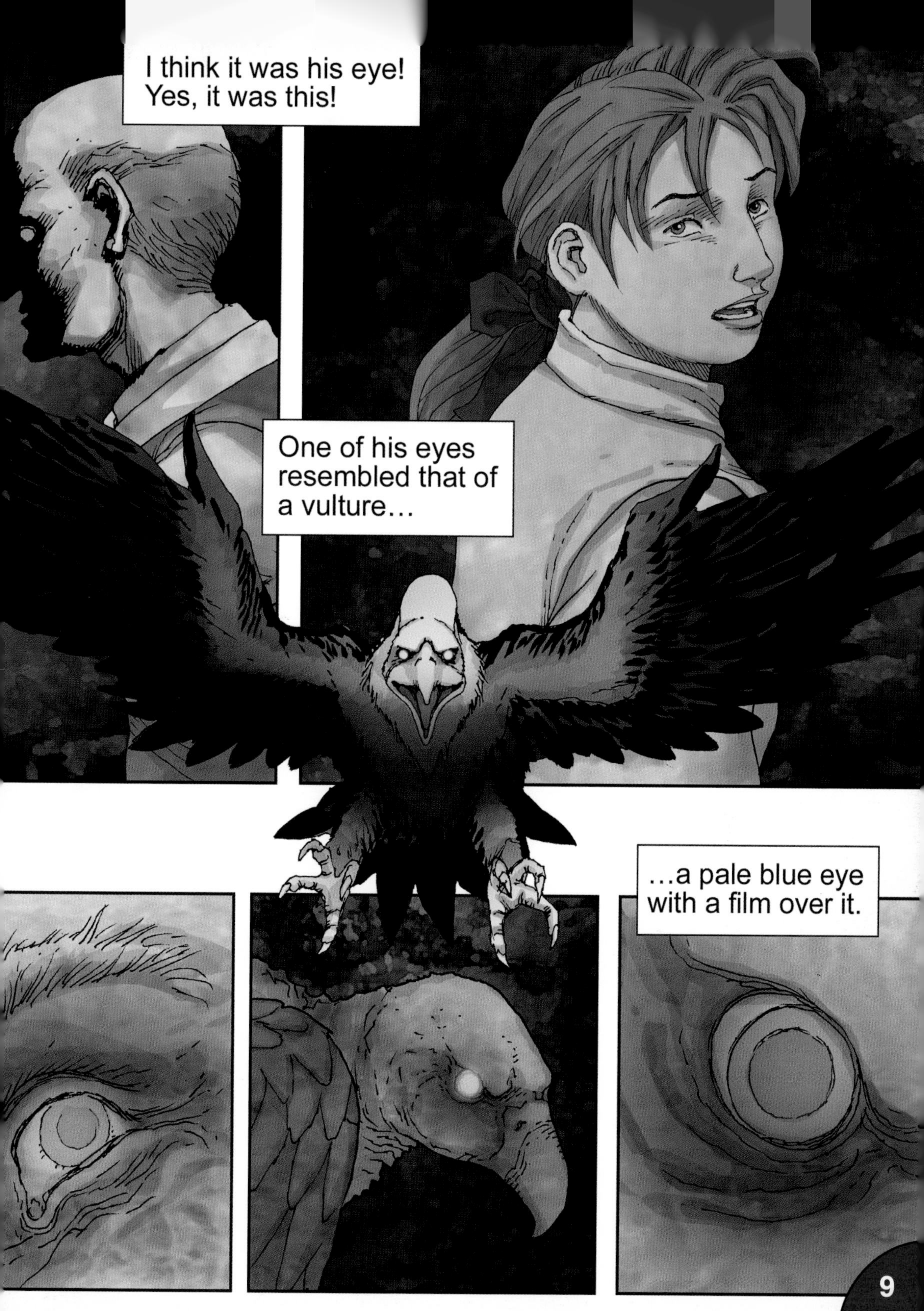
I think it was his eye!
Yes, it was this!
One of his eyes
resembled that of
a vulture…
…a pale blue eye
with a film over it.

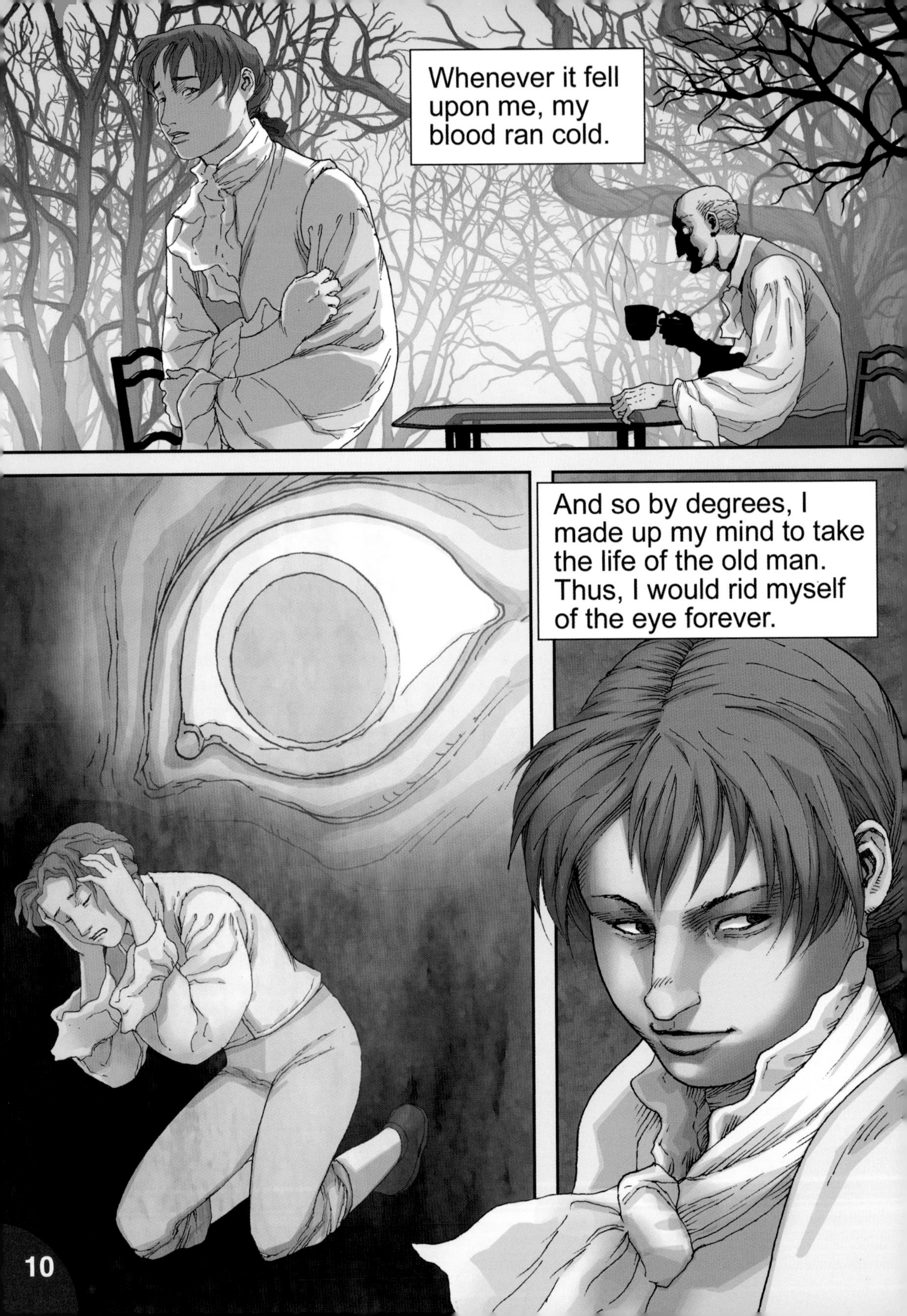
Whenever it fell upon me, my blood ran cold.
And so by degrees, I made up my mind to take the life of the old man. Thus, I would rid myself of the eye forever.

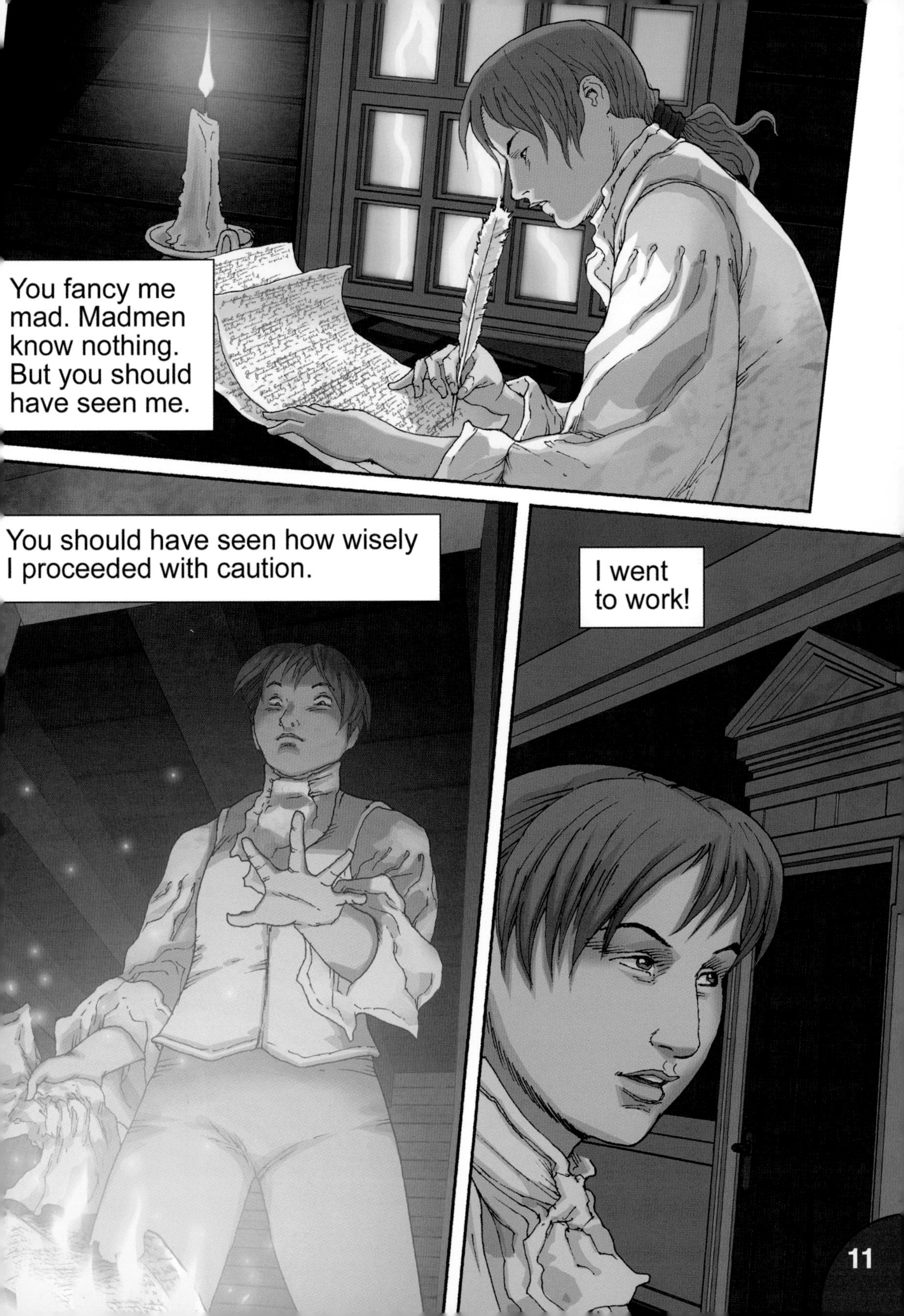
You fancy me mad. Madmen know nothing. But you should have seen me.
You should have seen how wisely I proceeded with caution.
I went to work!

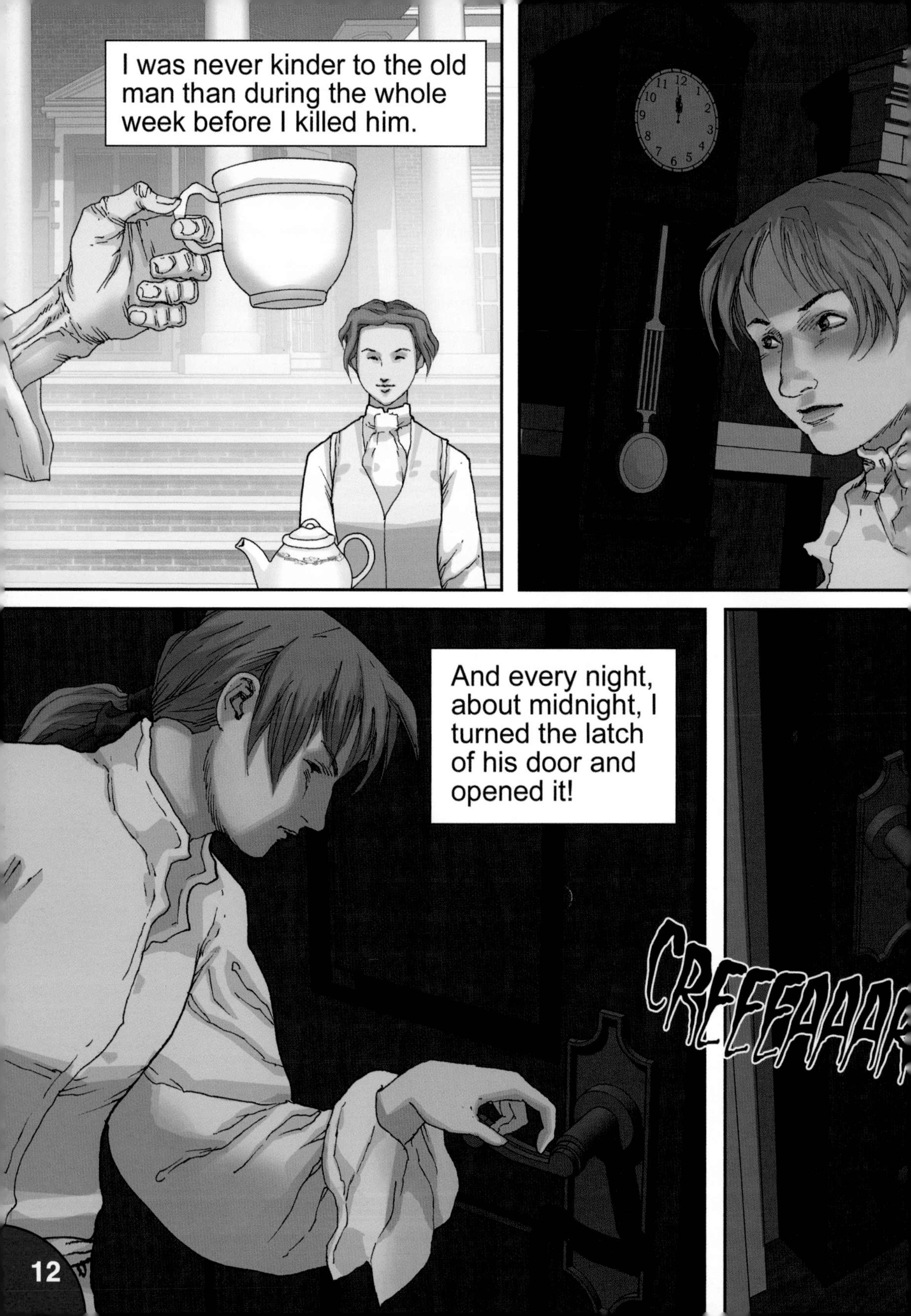
I was never kinder to the old man than during the whole week before I killed him.
And every night, about midnight, I turned the latch of his door and opened it!
CREEEAAAR

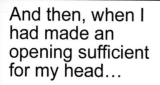

And then, when I had made an opening sufficient for my head…

…I put in a dark lantern and I thrust in my head. Oh, you would have laughed to see how cunningly I thrust it in! I moved it very slowly, so that I might not wake the old man.

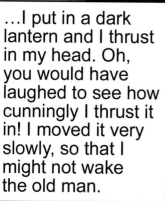

It took me an hour to place my whole head within the opening. Ha! Would a madman have been so wise as this?

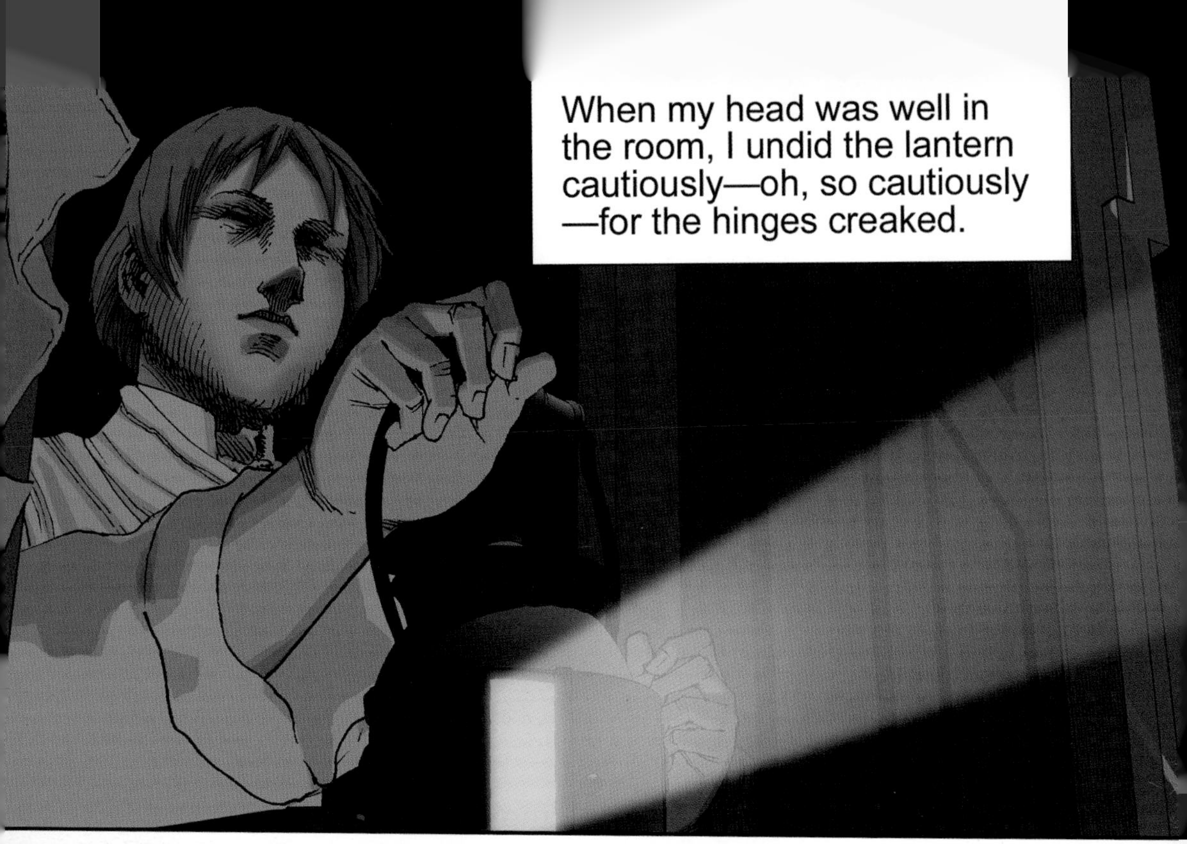
When my head was well in the room, I undid the lantern cautiously—oh, so cautiously —for the hinges creaked.

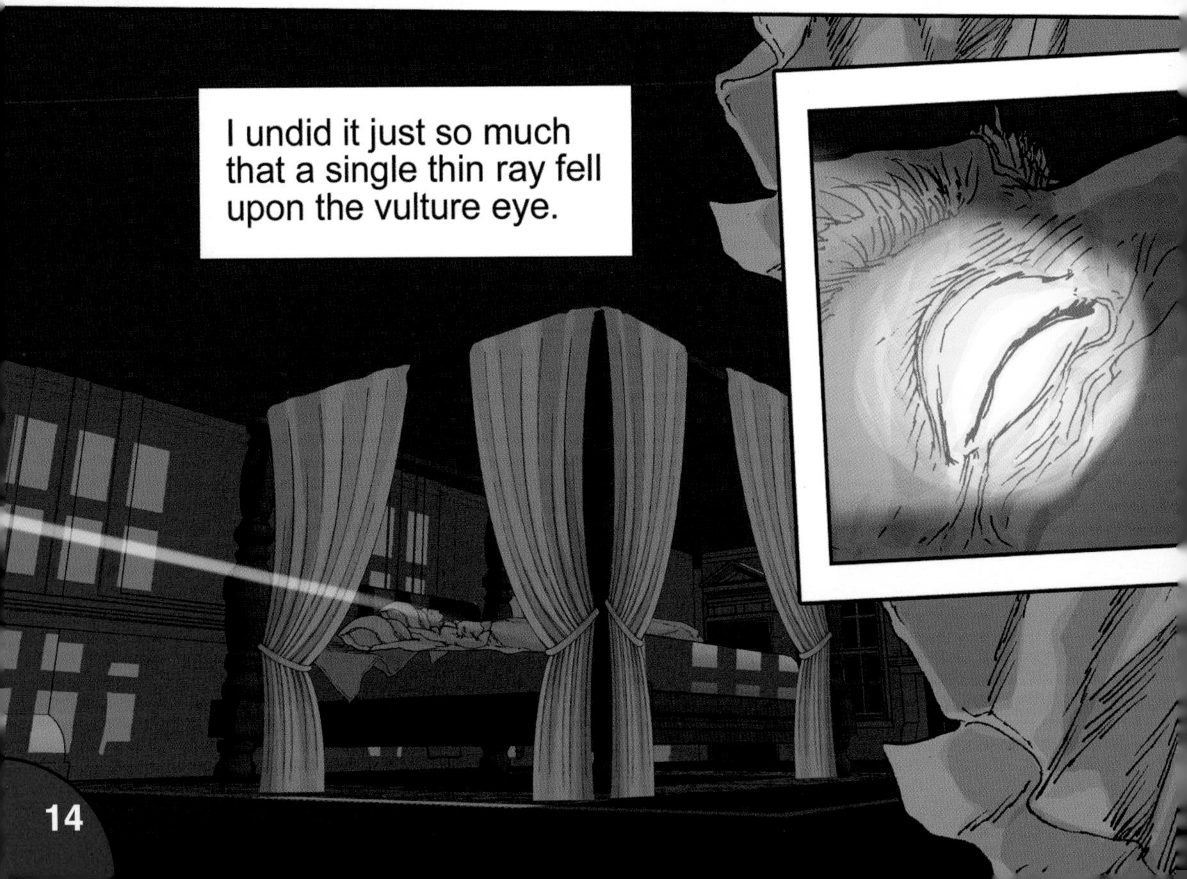
I undid it just so much that a single thin ray fell upon the vulture eye.

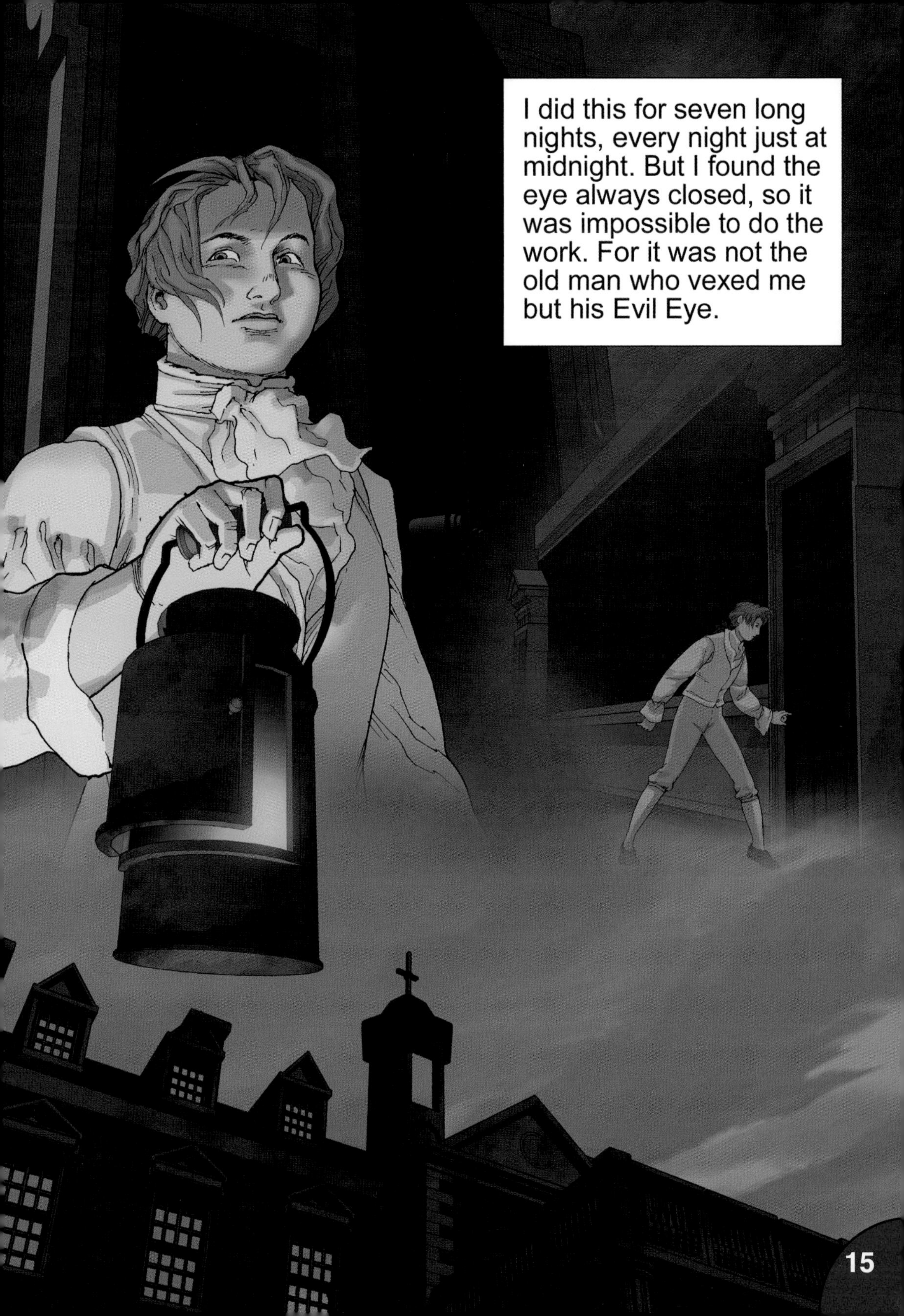
I did this for seven long nights, every night just at midnight. But I found the eye always closed, so it was impossible to do the work. For it was not the old man who vexed me but his Evil Eye.

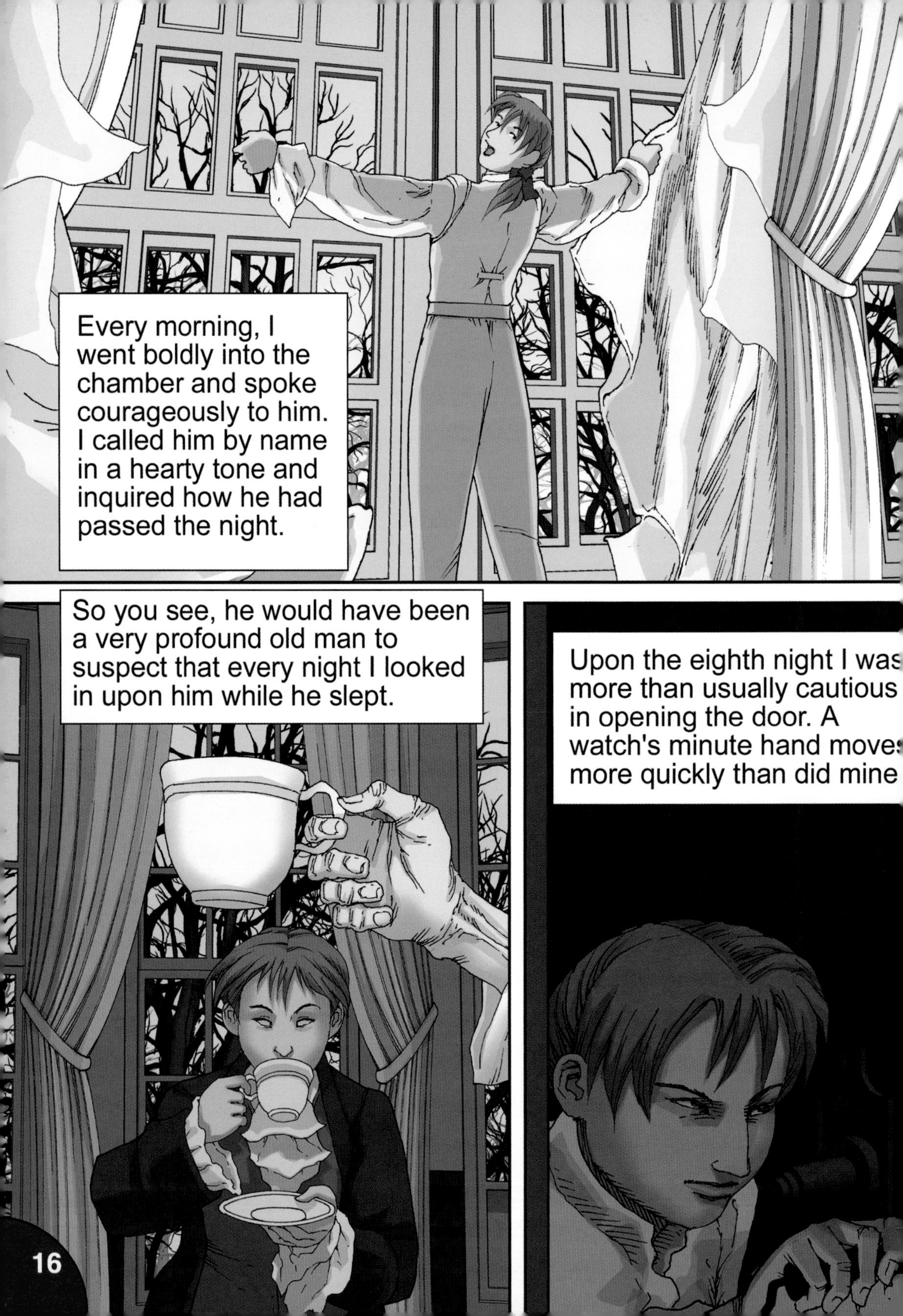
Every morning, I went boldly into the chamber and spoke courageously to him. I called him by name in a hearty tone and inquired how he had passed the night.
So you see, he would have been a very profound old man to suspect that every night I looked in upon him while he slept.
Upon the eighth night I was more than usually cautious in opening the door. A watch's minute hand moves more quickly than did mine

could scarcely contain my feelings of triumph. To think that he not even dreamed of my secret deeds or thoughts.

I chuckled at the idea, and perhaps he heard me, for he moved on the bed suddenly. Now you may think that I drew back, but no.

His room was as black as pitch, and I knew that he could not see the opening of the door. I kept pushing it on steadily, steadily.

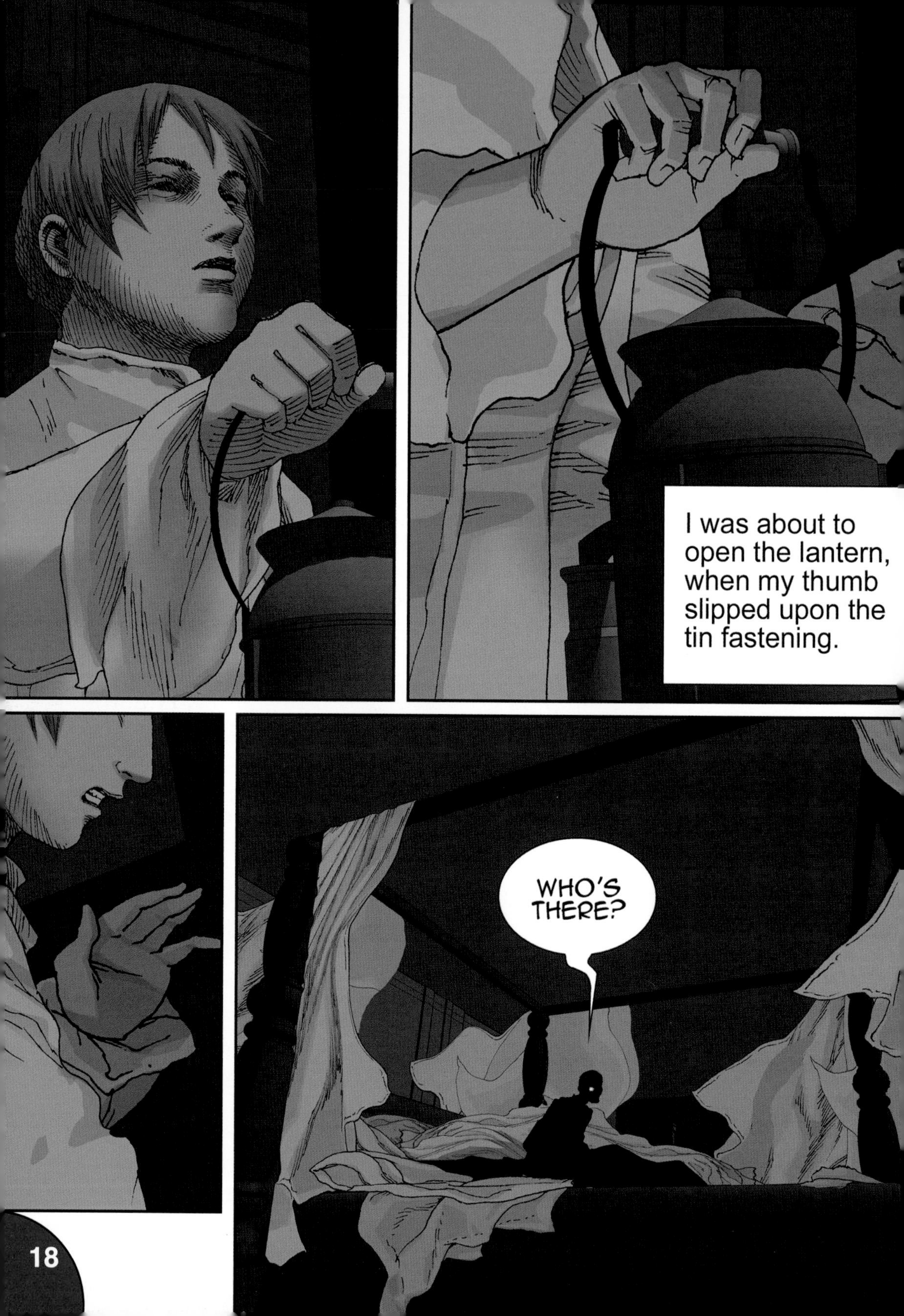
I was about to open the lantern, when my thumb slipped upon the tin fastening.
WHO'S THERE?

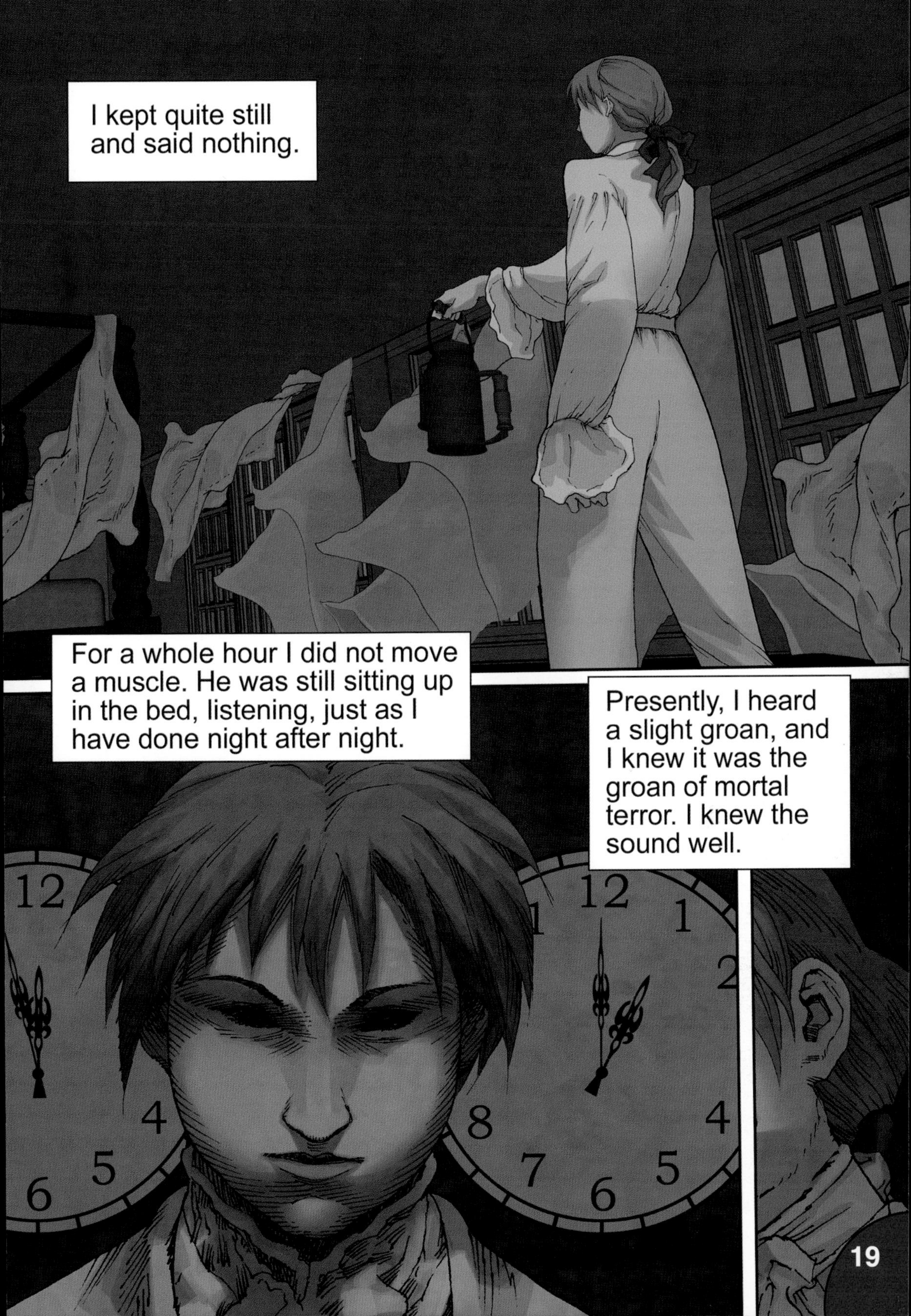
I kept quite still and said nothing.
For a whole hour I did not move a muscle. He was still sitting up in the bed, listening, just as I have done night after night.
Presently, I heard a slight groan, and I knew it was the groan of mortal terror. I knew the sound well.

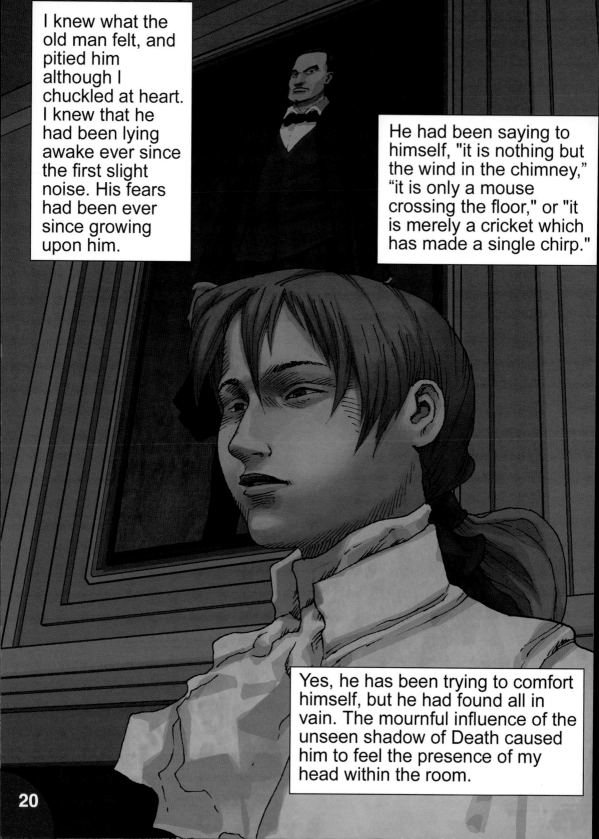

I knew what the old man felt, and pitied him although I chuckled at heart. I knew that he had been lying awake ever since the first slight noise. His fears had been ever since growing upon him.

He had been saying to himself, "it is nothing but the wind in the chimney," "it is only a mouse crossing the floor," or "it is merely a cricket which has made a single chirp."

Yes, he has been trying to comfort himself, but he had found all in vain. The mournful influence of the unseen shadow of Death caused him to feel the presence of my head within the room.

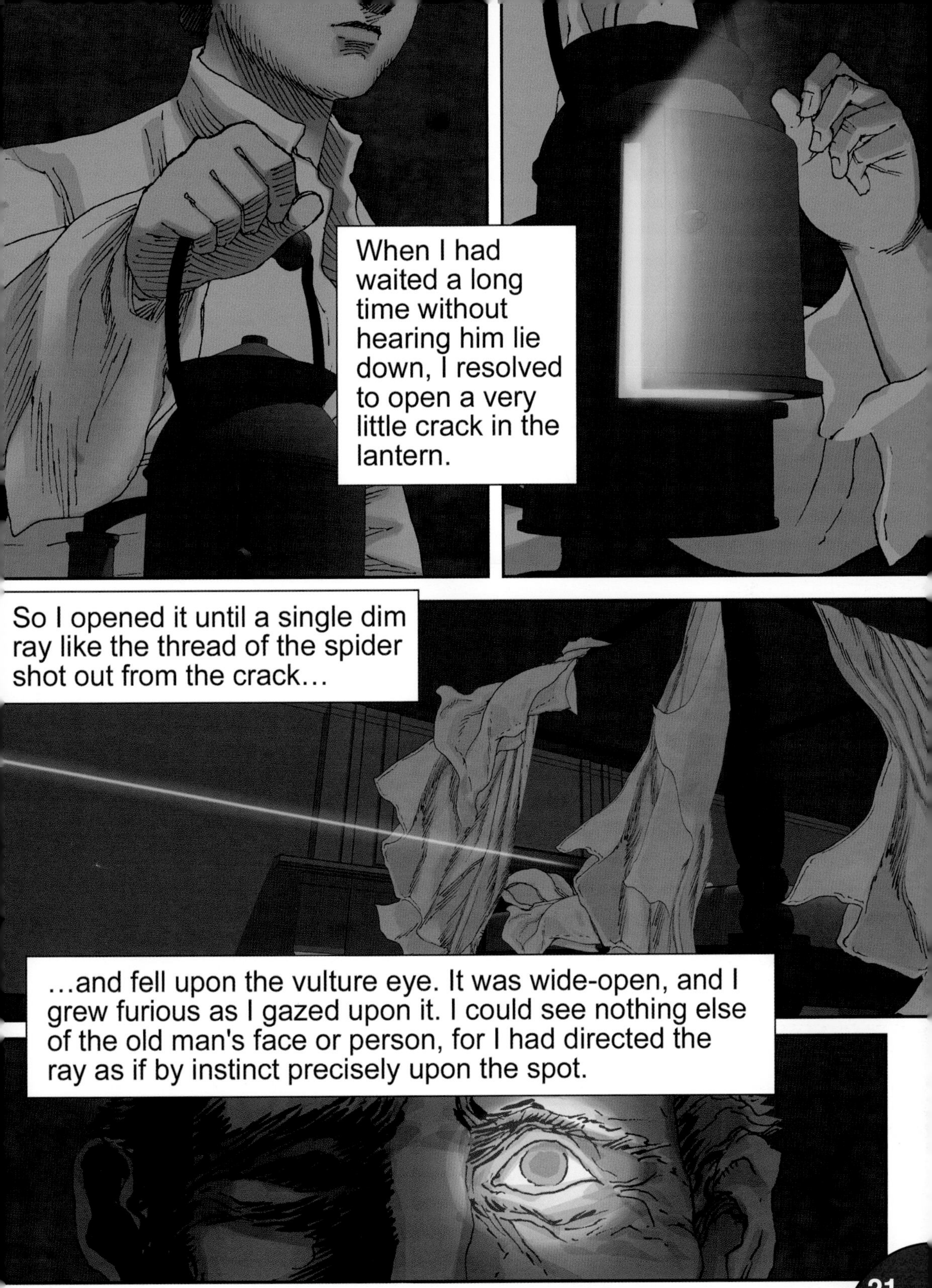
When I had waited a long time without hearing him lie down, I resolved to open a very little crack in the lantern.
So I opened it until a single dim ray like the thread of the spider shot out from the crack...
...and fell upon the vulture eye. It was wide-open, and I grew furious as I gazed upon it. I could see nothing else of the old man's face or person, for I had directed the ray as if by instinct precisely upon the spot.

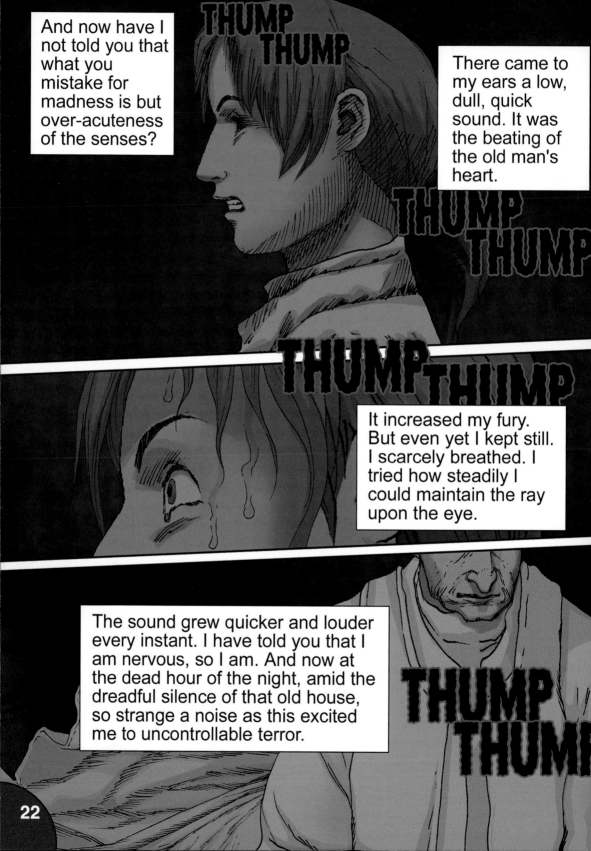

And now have I not told you that what you mistake for madness is but over-acuteness of the senses?

THUMP THUMP

There came to my ears a low, dull, quick sound. It was the beating of the old man's heart.

THUMP THUMP

THUMP THUMP

It increased my fury. But even yet I kept still. I scarcely breathed. I tried how steadily I could maintain the ray upon the eye.

The sound grew quicker and louder every instant. I have told you that I am nervous, so I am. And now at the dead hour of the night, amid the dreadful silence of that old house, so strange a noise as this excited me to uncontrollable terror.

THUMP THUMP

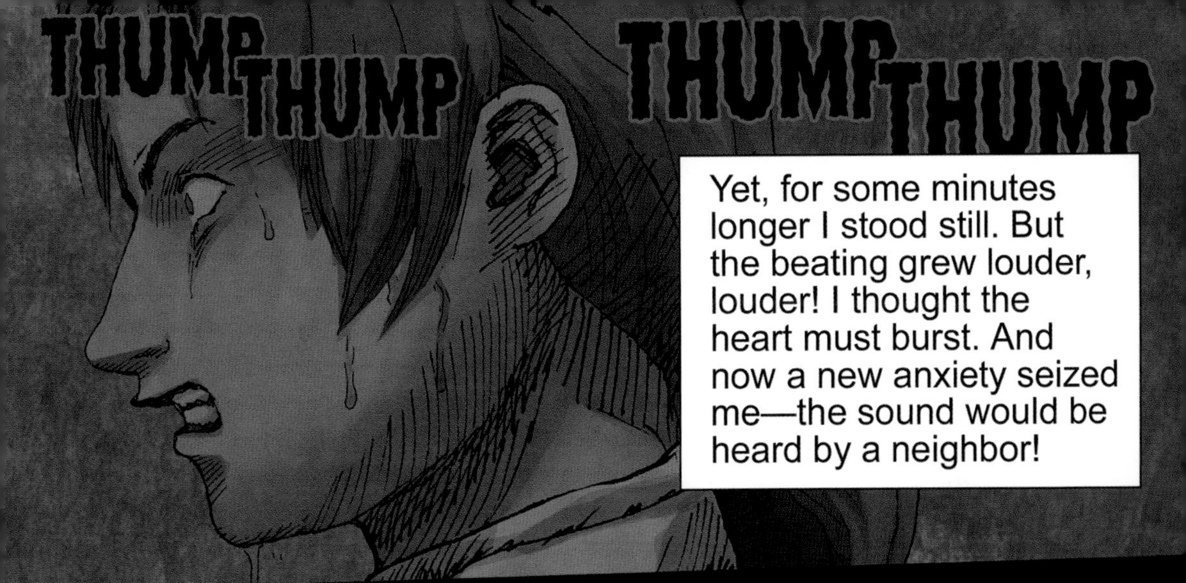
THUMP THUMP THUMP THUMP
Yet, for some minutes longer I stood still. But the beating grew louder, louder! I thought the heart must burst. And now a new anxiety seized me—the sound would be heard by a neighbor!

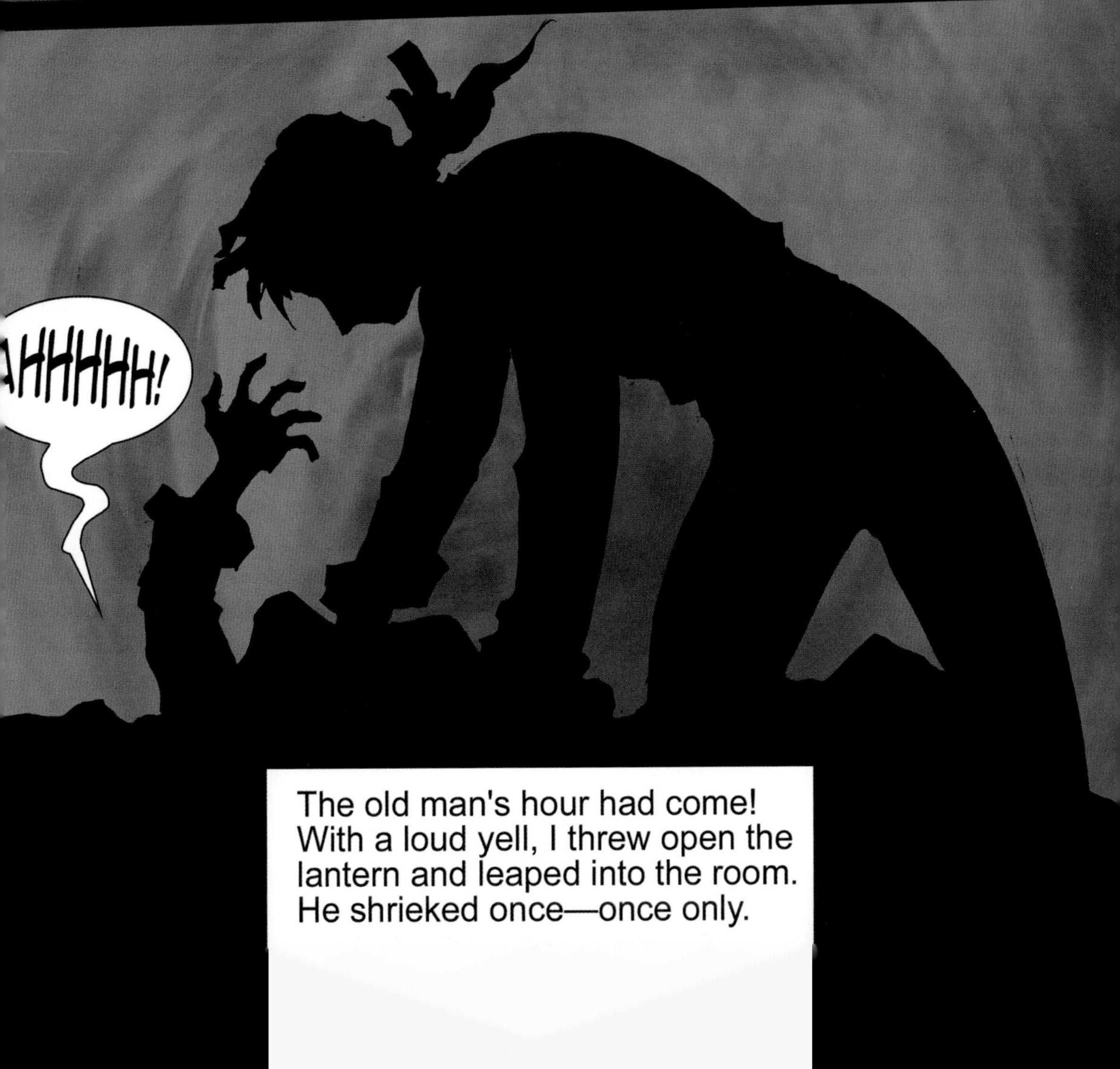
HHHHH!
The old man's hour had come! With a loud yell, I threw open the lantern and leaped into the room. He shrieked once—once only.

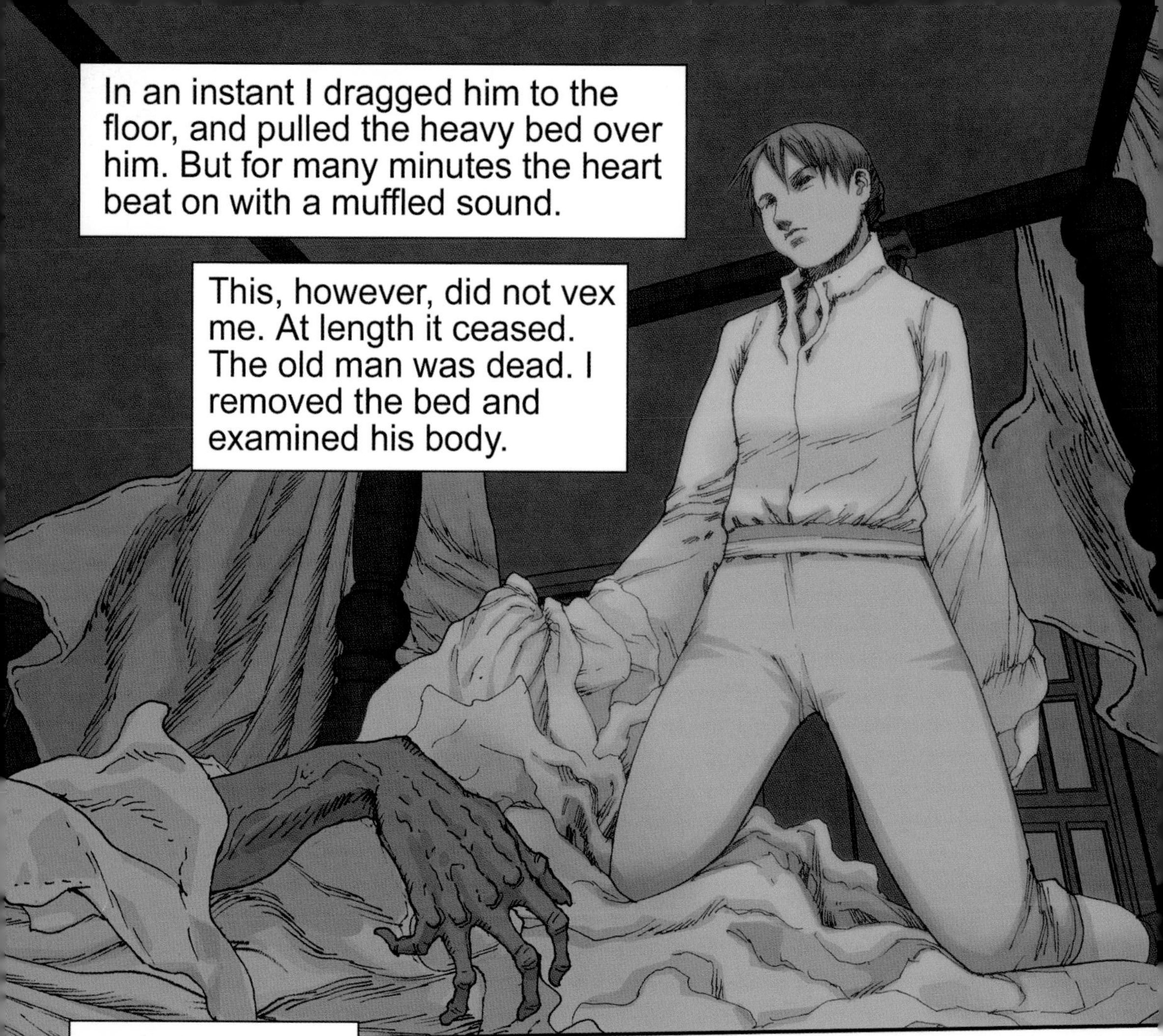
In an instant I dragged him to the floor, and pulled the heavy bed over him. But for many minutes the heart beat on with a muffled sound.
This, however, did not vex me. At length it ceased. The old man was dead. I removed the bed and examined his body.

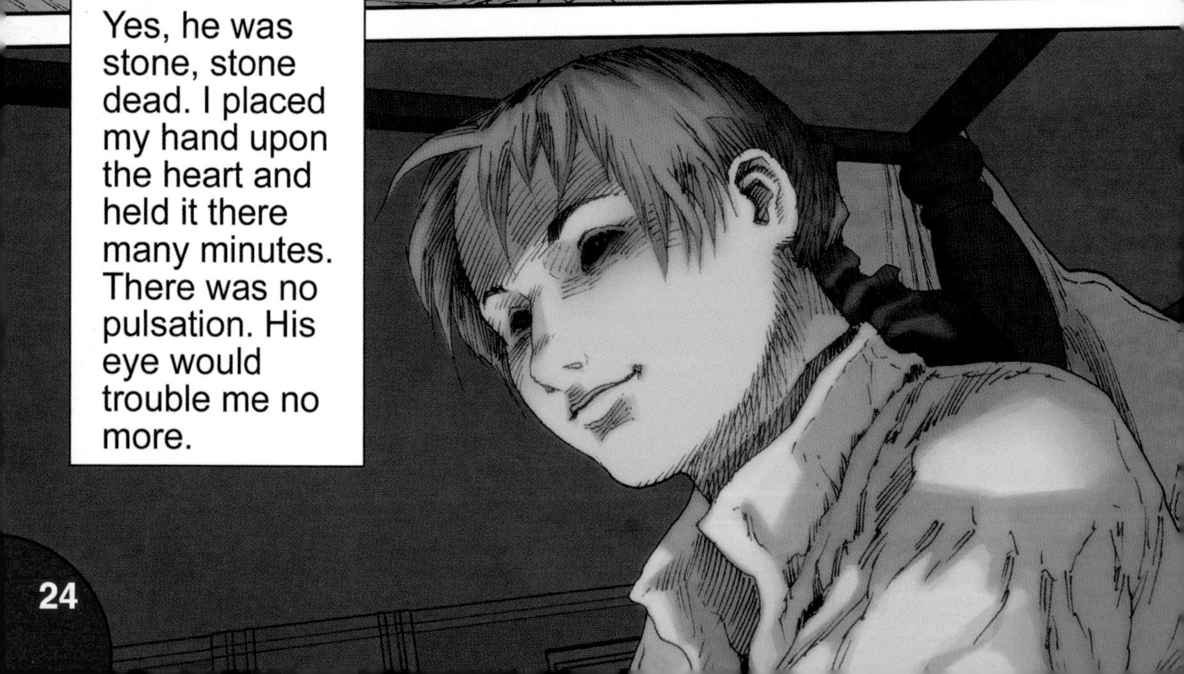
Yes, he was stone, stone dead. I placed my hand upon the heart and held it there many minutes. There was no pulsation. His eye would trouble me no more.

still you think me
mad, you will think
so no longer when I
describe the wise
precautions I took
to hide the body.

I worked
hastily, but
in silence.

I took up three planks from
the flooring of the parlor,
and deposited all between
the scantlings.

I then replaced the boards so
cleverly that no human eye
—not even his—could have
detected anything wrong.

When I had made an
end of these labors, it
was four o'clock—still
dark as midnight.

As the bell
sounded the
hour, there came
a knocking at the
street door.

KNOCK
KNOCK

25

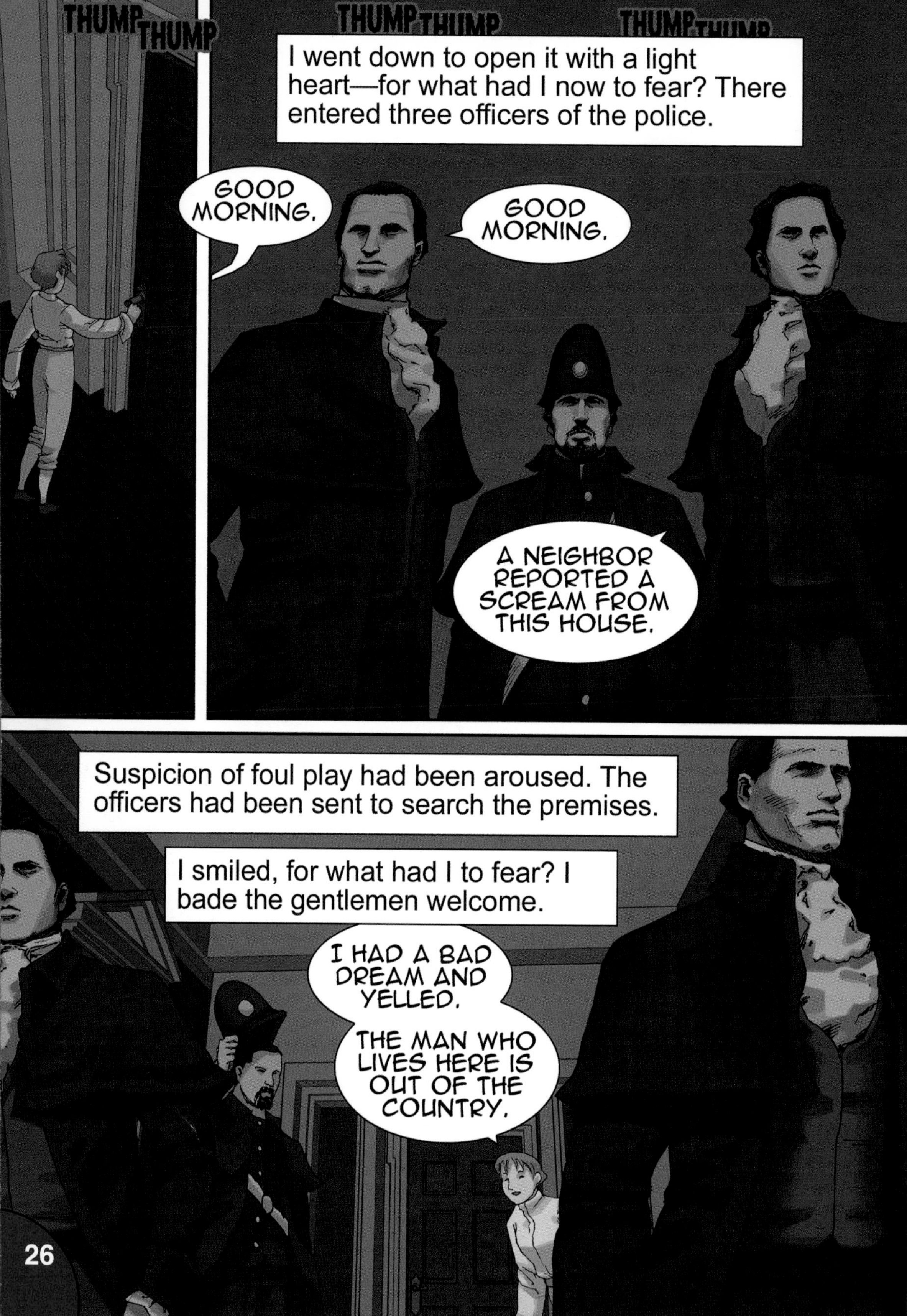
THUMP THUMP
THUMP THUMP
THUMP
I went down to open it with a light heart—for what had I now to fear? There entered three officers of the police.
GOOD MORNING.
GOOD MORNING.
A NEIGHBOR REPORTED A SCREAM FROM THIS HOUSE.
Suspicion of foul play had been aroused. The officers had been sent to search the premises.
I smiled, for what had I to fear? I bade the gentlemen welcome.
I HAD A BAD DREAM AND YELLED.
THE MAN WHO LIVES HERE IS OUT OF THE COUNTRY.

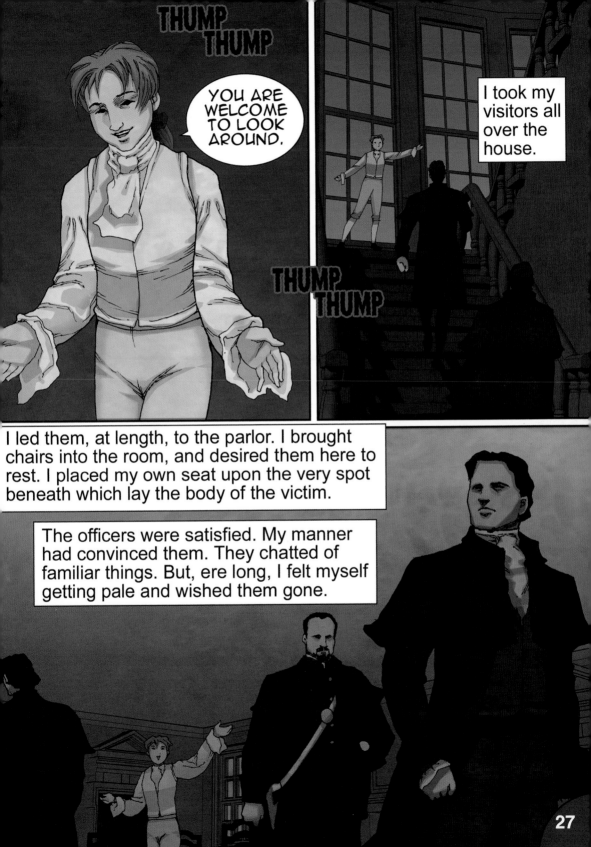

THUMP
THUMP

YOU ARE WELCOME TO LOOK AROUND.

THUMP
THUMP

I took my visitors all over the house.

I led them, at length, to the parlor. I brought chairs into the room, and desired them here to rest. I placed my own seat upon the very spot beneath which lay the body of the victim.

The officers were satisfied. My manner had convinced them. They chatted of familiar things. But, ere long, I felt myself getting pale and wished them gone.

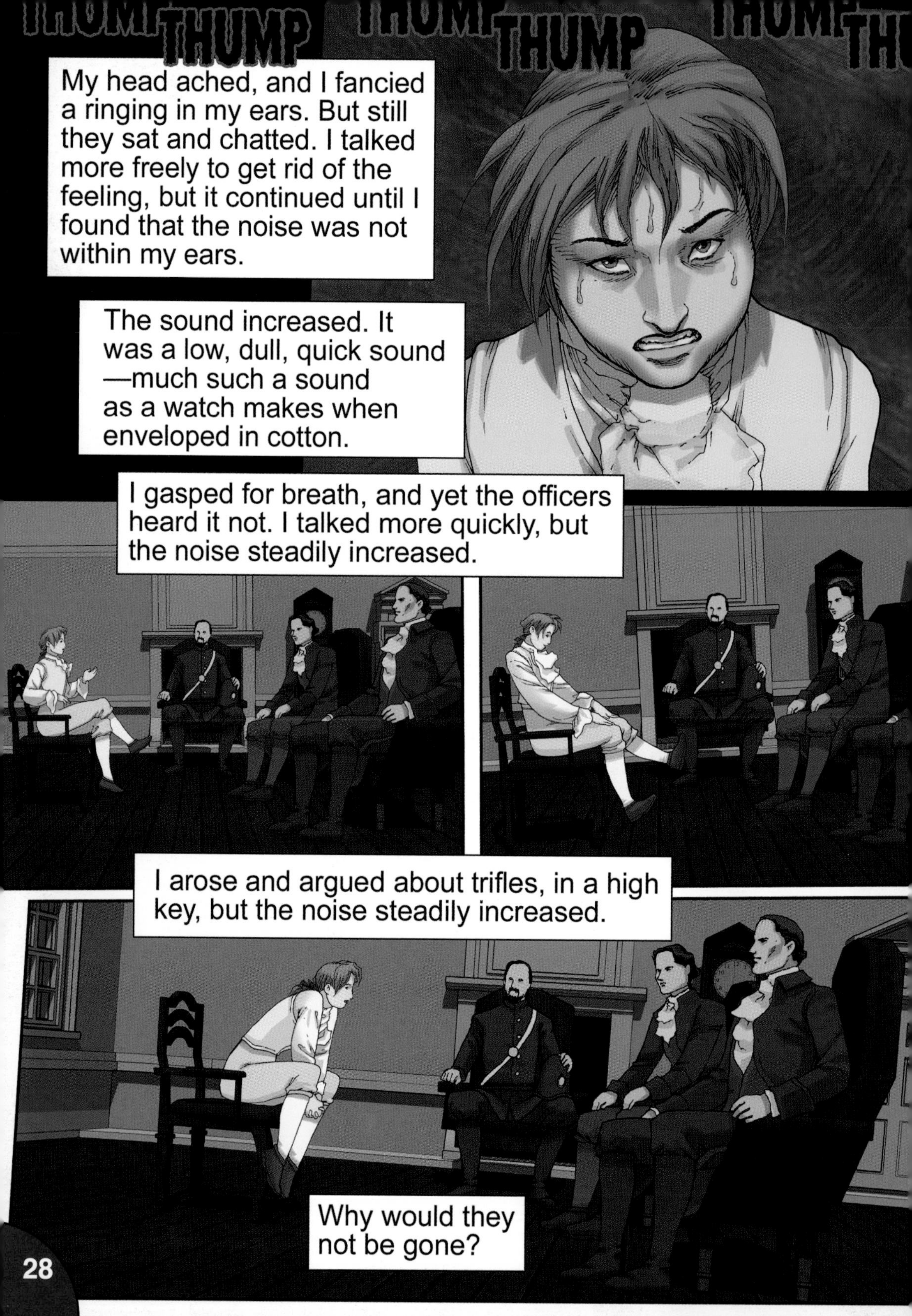
THUMP
THUMP
THUMP
My head ached, and I fancied a ringing in my ears. But still they sat and chatted. I talked more freely to get rid of the feeling, but it continued until I found that the noise was not within my ears.
The sound increased. It was a low, dull, quick sound —much such a sound as a watch makes when enveloped in cotton.
I gasped for breath, and yet the officers heard it not. I talked more quickly, but the noise steadily increased.
I arose and argued about trifles, in a high key, but the noise steadily increased.
Why would they not be gone?

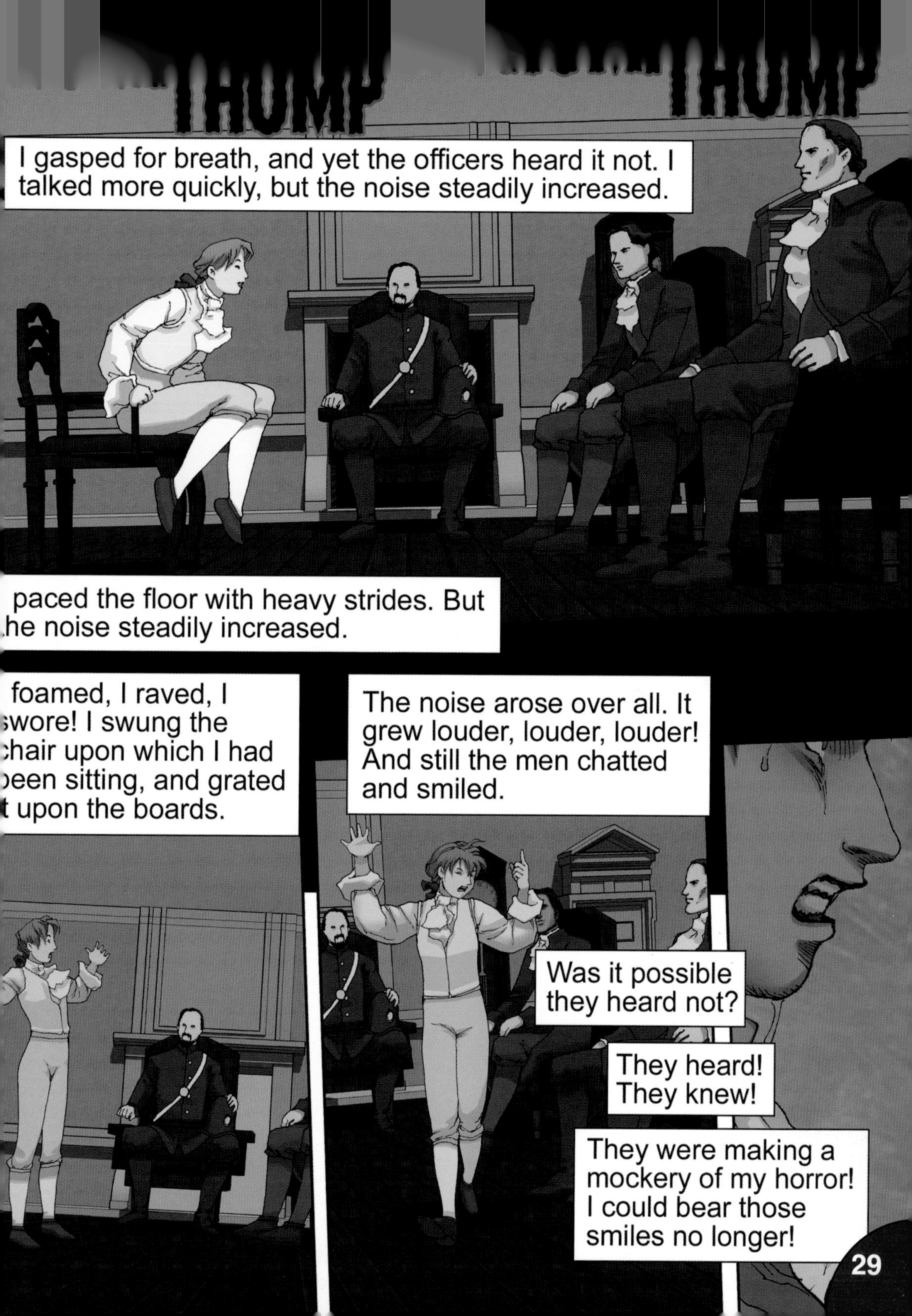
THUMP
THUMP
I gasped for breath, and yet the officers heard it not. I talked more quickly, but the noise steadily increased.
paced the floor with heavy strides. But he noise steadily increased.
foamed, I raved, I wore! I swung the hair upon which I had een sitting, and grated upon the boards.
The noise arose over all. It grew louder, louder, louder! And still the men chatted and smiled.
Was it possible they heard not?
They heard! They knew!
They were making a mockery of my horror! I could bear those smiles no longer!

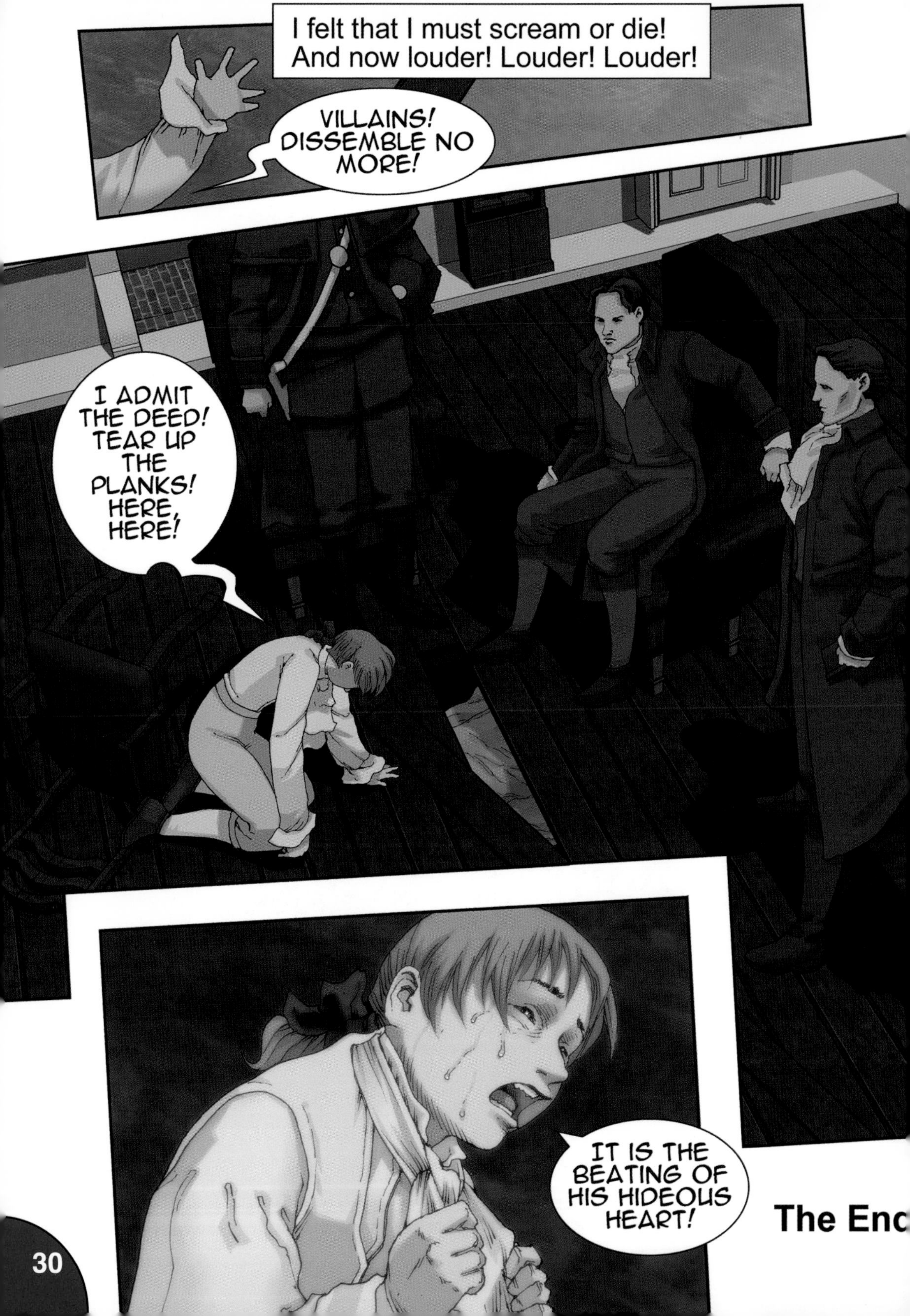
I felt that I must scream or die!
And now louder! Louder! Louder!
VILLAINS! DISSEMBLE NO MORE!
I ADMIT THE DEED! TEAR UP THE PLANKS! HERE, HERE!
IT IS THE BEATING OF HIS HIDEOUS HEART!

The Enc

About the Author

Edgar Allan Poe was born on January 19, 1809, in Boston, Massachusetts. His parents, Elizabeth Arnold Poe and David Poe Jr., were both actors. After his mother died in 1811, Edgar lived with his godfather John Allan in Richmond, Virginia. He was later sent to England and Scotland for schooling. In 1826, he attended the University of Virginia for 11 months.

In 1827, Poe published a pamphlet of poems. He then joined the army under the name Edgar A. Perry. Two years later, Allan purchased Poe's release from the army and got him into the U.S. Military Academy at West Point. Poe was expelled from West Point in 1831, and his education ended.

Poe continued to write poetry and eventually short stories filled with terror and sadness. He won several prizes for his writing. By 1835, Poe had become an editor at a magazine in Richmond. The next year, he married his young cousin Virginia Clemm.

Early on, Poe made a name for himself as a critical reviewer. He held several different editing jobs throughout his life. But, it wasn't until his poem "The Raven" was published in 1845 that he became famous.

Poe died on October 7, 1849, in Baltimore, Maryland. Today, Edgar Allan Poe is often remembered for his tales of mystery and death. He remains an important influence on many writers.

Additional Works

The Fall of the House of Usher (1839)
The Gold Bug (1843)
The Tell-Tale Heart (1843)
The Raven (1845)
The Cask of Amontillado (1846)
Eureka (1848)
Annabel Lee (1849)

Glossary

acute – feeling or experiencing something even though it is barely preser

dissemble – to pretend or hide one's true intentions.

fancy – to believe without being certain.

hideous – extremely ugly.

parlor – a private room for entertaining guests.

precaution – something done before an event.

profound – having intelligence and insight.

scantling – a small piece of lumber.

trifle – something of little or no importance.

Web Sites

To learn more about Edgar Allan Poe, visit the ABDO Group online at **www.abdopublishing.com**. Web sites about Poe are featured on our Bool Links page. These links are routinely monitored and updated to provide the most current information available.